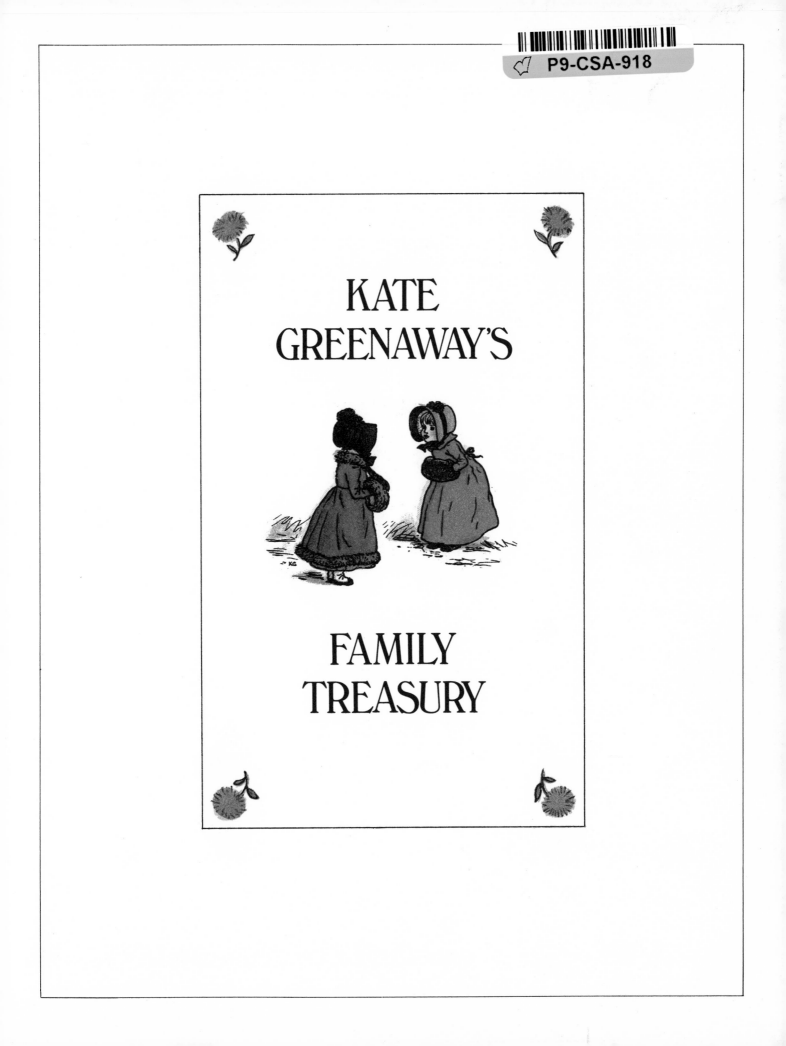

KATE GREENAWAY'S

FAMILY TREASURY

KATE GREENAWAY'S FAMILY TREASURY

Selections from Kate Greenaway's
A Applepie,
Under the Window,
Mother Goose,
Book of Games,
and Marigold Garden

Derrydale Books · New York

Special material copyright © MCMLXXIX by Crown Publishers, Inc.
All rights reserved.
This edition is published by Derrydale Books,
a division of Crown Publishers, Inc.
a b c d e f g h
DERRYDALE 1979 EDITION
Manufactured in the United States of America

Design by Lauren Dong

Library of Congress Cataloging in Publication Data

Greenaway, Kate, 1846-1901.
    Kate Greenaway's Family treasury.

    SUMMARY: Five of Kate Greenaway's most famous
books: "A Apple Pie," "Book of Games," "Marigold
Garden," "Mother Goose," and "Under the Window."
    1. Children's literature, English. [1. Litera-
ture—Collections. 2. Alphabet. 3. Games.
4. English poetry. 5. Nursery rhymes] I. Title.
II. Title: Family treasury.
PZ5.G725Kat 1979 [E] 79-16363
ISBN 0-517-29308-0

FOREWORD

Kate Greenaway has a special place in the annals of children's book illustration. Other artists have matched her degree of charm, simplicity, and delicacy, but Kate Greenaway managed to give us all these from a child's viewpoint. The postures and facial expressions of her children are indeed childlike, and not just "adult" appreciations of childish cuteness. When her children run, they run with impetuosity and glee. They skip and play in a world of their own. We have all, of course, been children. But Kate Greenaway not only observed children: she remembered what it feels like to be a child.

Kate Greenaway was born in 1846 in the town of Hoxton, England, and grew up there. According to her own report, it was much like the villages depicted in her illustrations; houses with thatched roofs, little gardens, and picket fences. She dressed her children in old-fashioned country outfits, not in the precious style of late nineteenth-century London. Not only did her art reflect her humble origins, but her lifestyle did as well. By the mid-1880s her works had received international acclaim, but she remained shy and retiring, avoiding public accolades.

It is difficult to call any of Kate Greenaway's work her best, so even is the quality of her entire output. But the five books selected for the present volume are surely representative. *Under the Window* (1878) was her first major success. The others appeared in this order: *Mother Goose* (1881); *Marigold Garden* (1885), for which Kate Greenaway wrote the verses herself; *A Apple Pie* (1886), and the *Book of Games* (1889). Although the five books cover a period of eleven years, there is no appreciable change in style. Arsène Alexandre, a French writer who was a contemporary of Kate Greenaway, described her as a "landscape artist, a master of the art of the smile, of the gaily naïve smile of an artless child." Like an English country landscape, Kate Greenaway's art has a feeling of eternal freshness to it. It is an art of childhood and springtime.

SOLOMON J. SCHEPPS

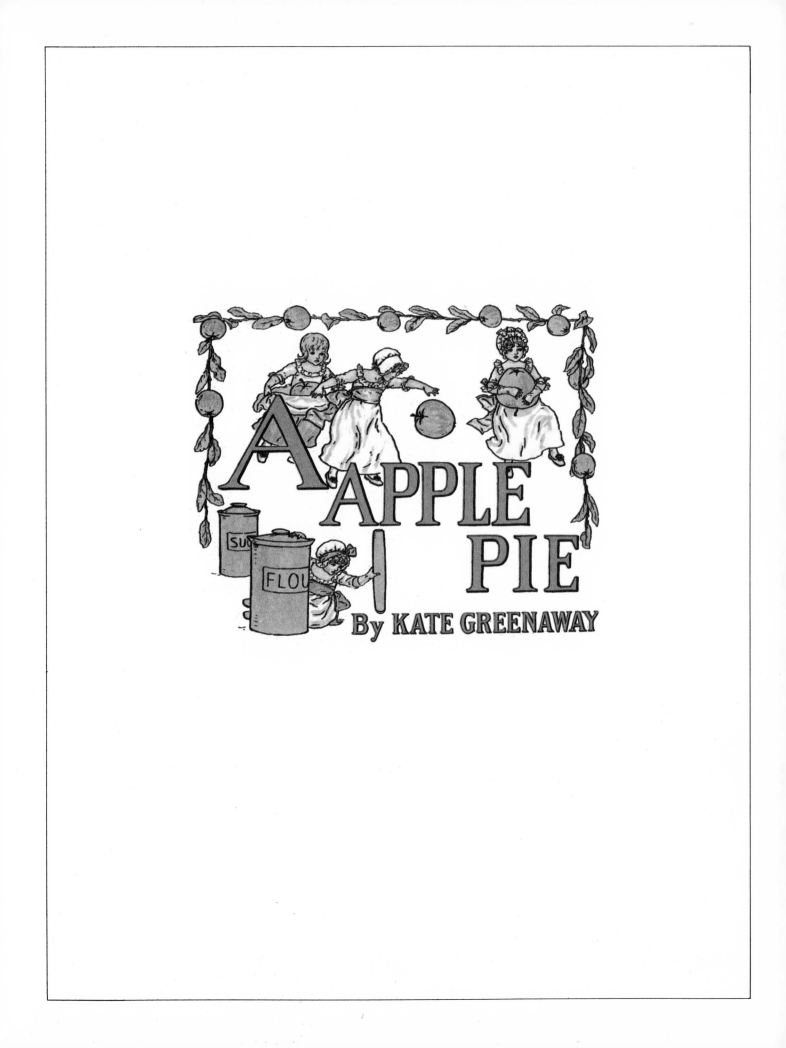

NOTE: on *A Apple Pie:*
The text for this book is a Mother Goose nursery rhyme. The Mother Goose poems first appeared in English in the early eighteenth century, when *i* and *j* were used interchangeably. Consequently, there is no *i* in the sequence.

A APPLE PIE

B BIT IT

C CUT IT

D DEALT IT

E EAT IT

F FOUGHT FOR IT

G GOT IT

H HAD IT

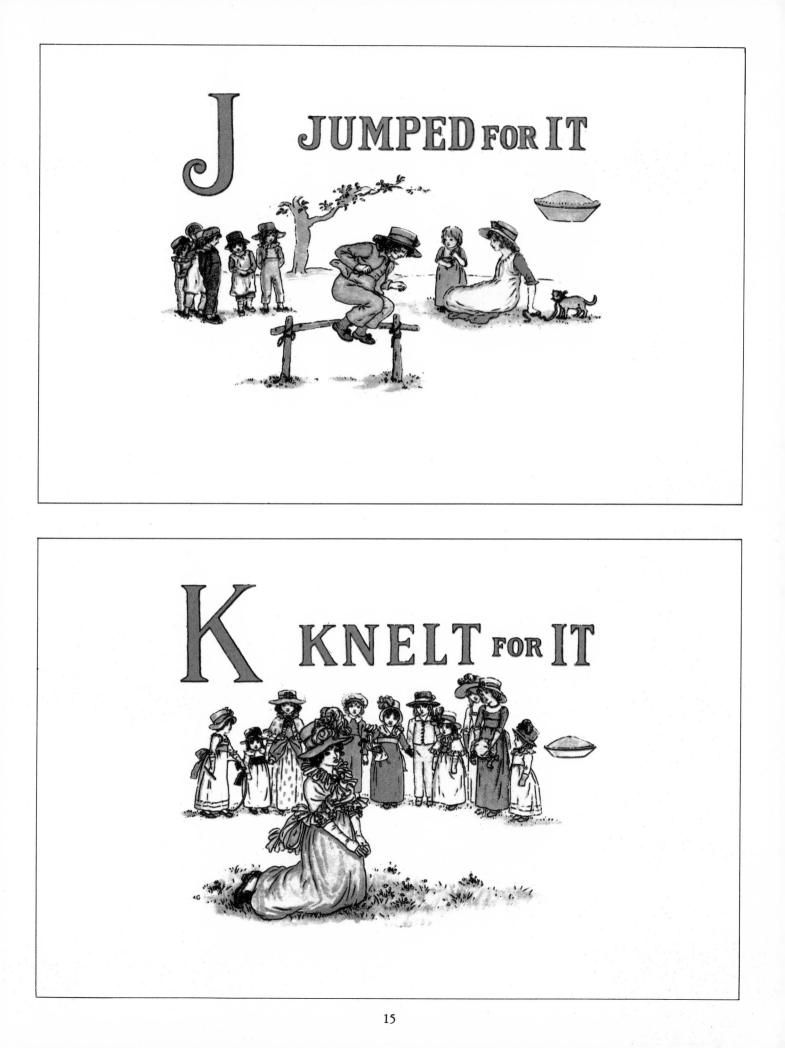

J JUMPED FOR IT

K KNELT FOR IT

L LONGED FOR IT

M MOURNED FOR IT

N NODDED FOR IT

O OPENED IT

P PEEPED IN IT

Q QUARTERED IT

R RAN FOR IT

S SANG FOR IT

T TOOK IT

UVWXYZ

ALL HAD A LARGE SLICE
AND WENT OFF TO
BED

UNDER THE WINDOW

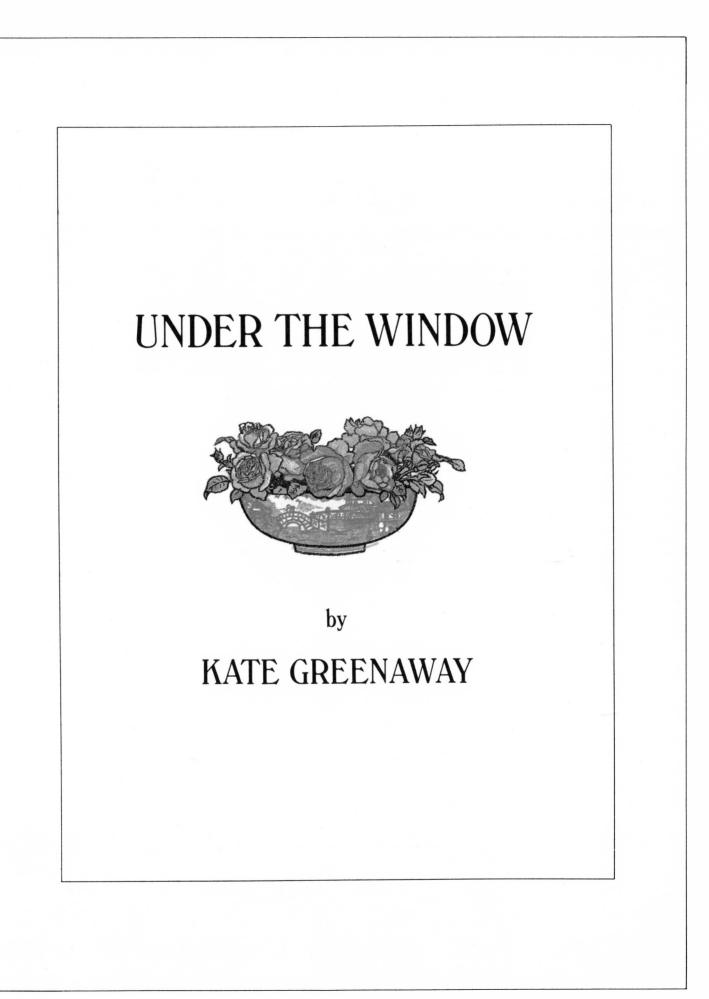

by

KATE GREENAWAY

THIS little fat Goblin,
   A notable sinner,
Stole cabbages daily,
   For breakfast and dinner.

The Farmer looked sorry;
   He cried, and with pain,
"That rogue has been here
   For his cabbage again!"

That little plump Goblin,
   He laughed, "Ho! ho! ha!
Before me he catches,
   He'll have to run far."

That little fat Goblin,
   He never need sorrow;
He stole three to-day,
   And he'll steal more to-morrow.

YES, that's the girl that struts about,
 She's very proud,—so very proud!
Her *bow-wow*'s quite as proud as she;
They both are very wrong to be
 So proud—so very proud.

See, Jane and Willy laugh at her,
 They say she's very proud;
Says Jane, "My stars!—they're very silly;"
"Indeed they are," cries little Willy,
 "To walk so stiff and proud."

AS I stepped out to hear the news,
I met a lass in socks and shoes;
She'd shoes with strings, and a friend had tied them,
She'd a nice little pair of feet inside them!

THREE tabbies took out their cats to tea,
As well-behaved tabbies as well could be:
Each sat in the chair that each preferred,
They mewed for their milk, and they sipped and purred.
Now tell me this (as these cats you've seen them)—
How many lives had these cats between them?

TOMMY was a silly boy.
   "I can fly," he said;
He started off, but very soon
   He tumbled on his head.

      His little sister Prue was there,
         To see how he would do it;
      She knew that, after all his boast,
         Full dearly Tom would rue it!

KG

BENEATH the lilies—tall, white garden lilies— | Ere long a Prince came riding in the sunshine,
The Princess slept, a charmed sleep alway; | A wind just swayed the lilies to and fro;
For ever were the fairy bluebells ringing, | It woke the Princess, tho' the bluebell music
For ever thro' the night and thro' the day. | Kept ringing, ringing, sleepily and low.

K.G.

LITTLE Miss Patty and Master Paul
Have found two snails on the garden wall.
"These snails," said Paul, "how slow they walk!—
A great deal slower than we can talk.
Make haste, Mr. Snail, travel quicker, I pray;
In a race with our tongues you'd be beaten to-day."

WHAT is Tommy running for,
      Running for,
      Running for?
What is Tommy running for,
   On this fine day?

Jimmy will run after Tommy,
      After Tommy,
      After Tommy;
That's what Tommy's running for,
   On this fine day.

INDEED it is true, it is perfectly true;
  Believe me, indeed, I am playing no tricks;
An old man and his dog bide up there in the moon,
  And he's cross as a bundle of sticks.

THE finest, biggest fish, you see,
Will be the trout that's caught by me;
But if the monster will not bite,
Why, then I'll hook a little mite.

PRINCE FINIKIN and his mamma
   Sat sipping their bohea;
"Good gracious!" said his Highness, "why,
   What girl is this I see?

"Most certainly it cannot be
  A native of our town;"
And he turned him round to his mamma,
  Who set her teacup down.

But Dolly simply looked at them,
  She did not speak a word;
"She has no voice," said Finikin;
  "It's really quite absurd."

Then Finikin's mamma observed,
  "Dear Prince, it seems to me,
She looks as if she'd like to drink
  A cup of my bohea."

So Finikin poured out her tea,
  And gave her currant-pie;
Then Finikin said, "Dear mamma,
  What a kind Prince am I!"

K.G

POOR Dicky's dead!—The bell we toll,
And lay him in the deep, dark hole.
The sun may shine, the clouds may rain,
But Dick will never pipe again!
His quilt will be as sweet as ours,—
Bright buttercups and cuckoo flowers.

"LITTLE Polly, will you go a-walking to-day?"
"Indeed, little Susan, I will, if I may."
"Little Polly, your mother has said you may go:
She was nice to say 'Yes;' she should never say 'No.'

"A rook has a nest on the top of the tree,—
A big ship is coming from over the sea:
Now, which would be nicest, the ship on the nest?"
"Why, that would be nicest that Polly likes best."

SOME geese went out a-walking,
    To breakfast and to dine;
They craned their necks, and plumed themselves—
    They numbered four from nine;
With their cackle, cackle, cackle!
    They thought themselves so fine.

A dame went walking by herself,
    A very ancient crone;
She said, "I wish that all you geese
    Were starved to skin and bone!
Do stop that cackle, cackle, now,
    And leave me here alone."

K.G

LOOK over the wall, and I'll tell you why,—
The King and the Queen will soon pass by;
Madams and masters, look this way,
The King and his Court ride past to-day.

The Queen has a robe that is gold and red,
She is stately, and sits with a crown on her head,
And four very little boys after her go,
To do as she bids them,—they never say "No."

The banners are waving, the soldiers are drumming;
'Tis indeed a fine sight that, I tell you, is coming!
So, if you look long enough over the wall,
You'll see a great deal, if you do not see all.

K.G.

LITTLE boys and girls, will you come and ride
With me on my broomstick,—far and wide?
First round the sun, then round the moon,
And we'll light on the steeple, to hear a merry tune.

K C

HEIGH HO!—time creeps but slow;
    I've looked up the hill so long;
None come this way, the sun sinks low,
    And my shadow's very long.

They said I should sail in a little boat,
    Up the stream, by the great white mill;
But I've waited all day, and none come my way,
    I've waited—I'm waiting still.

They said I should see a fairy town,
    With houses all of gold,
And silver people, and a gold church steeple;—
    But it wasn't the truth they told.

"FOR what are you longing, you three little boys?
    Oh, what would you like to eat?"
"We should like some apples, or gingerbread,—
    Or a fine big drum to beat."

"Oh, what will you give me, you three little boys,
    In exchange for these good, good things?"
"Some bread and cheese, and some radishes,
    And our little brown bird that sings."

"Now, that won't do, you three little chums,
    I'll have something better than that,—
Two of your fingers, and two of your thumbs,
    In the crown of your largest hat!"

YES, it is sad of them—
    Shocking to me;
Bad,—yes, it's bad of them,—
    Bad of all three.

Warnings they've had from me,
    Still I repeat them,—
Cold is the water—the
    Fishes will eat them.

Yet they will row about,
    Tho' I say "Fie!" to them;
Fathers may scold at it,
    Mothers may cry to them.

K.G

WHICH is the way to Somewhere Town?
   Oh, up in the morning early;
Over the tiles and the chimney-pots,
   That is the way, quite clearly.

And which is the door to Somewhere Town?
   Oh, up in the morning early;
The round red sun is the door to go through,
   That is the way, quite clearly.

BOWL away! bowl away!
    Fast as you can;
He who can fastest bowl,
    He is my man!

Up and down, round about,—
    Don't let it fall;
Ten times, or twenty times,
    Beat, beat them all!

"SHALL I sing?" says the Lark,
    "Shall I bloom?" says the Flower;
"Shall I come?" says the Sun,
    "Or shall I?" says the Shower.

Sing your song, pretty Bird,
    Roses, bloom for an hour;
Shine on, dearest Sun,
    Go away, naughty Shower!

THREE little girls were sitting on a rail,
    Sitting on a rail,
    Sitting on a rail;
Three little girls were sitting on a rail,
    On a fine hot day in September.

What did they talk about that fine day,
    That fine day,
    That fine day?
What did they talk about that fine day,—
    That fine hot day in September?

The crows and the corn they talked about,
    Talked about,
    Talked about;
But nobody knows what was said by the crows,
    On that fine hot day in September.

OH, what has the old man come for?
Oh, what has the old man come for?
   To run away with Billy, I say,
And that's what the old man has come for.

Ah, what will Billy's mamma say?
Ah, what will Billy's papa say?
   What a dreadful fright
   They'll be in to-night!—
Oh, what will papa and mamma say?

LITTLE baby, if I threw
This fair blossom down to you,
Would you catch it as you stand,
Holding up each tiny hand,
Looking out of those grey eyes,
Where such deep, deep wonder lies?

KG

UNDER the window is my garden,
  Where sweet, sweet flowers grow;
And in the pear-tree dwells a robin,
  The dearest bird I know.

Tho' I peep out betimes in the morning,
  Still the flowers are up the first;
Then I try and talk to the robin,
  And perhaps he'd chat—if he durst.

WILL you be my little wife,
  If I ask you? Do!—
I'll buy you such a Sunday frock,
  A nice umbrella, too.

And you shall have a little hat,
  With such a long white feather,
A pair of gloves, and sandal shoes,
  The softest kind of leather.

And you shall have a tiny house,
  A beehive full of bees,
A little cow, a largish cat,
  And green sage cheese.

I SAW a ship that sailed the sea,
   It left me as the sun went down;
The white birds flew, and followed it
   To town—to London town.

Right sad were we to stand alone,
   And see it pass so far away;
And yet we knew some ship would come—
   Some other ship—some other day.

KATE
GREENAWAY'S
MOTHER GOOSE

or the

OLD NURSERY
RHYMES

HARK! hark! the dogs bark,
The beggars are coming to town;
Some in rags and some in tags,
And some in silken gowns.
Some gave them white bread,
And some gave them brown,
And some gave them a good horse-whip,
And sent them out of the town.

47

WE'RE all jolly boys, and we're coming
with a noise,
Our stockings shall be made
Of the finest silk,
And our tails shall touch the ground.

GEORGIE Peorgie, pudding and pie,
Kissed the girls and made them cry;
When the girls began to play,
Georgie Peorgie runs away.

DAFFY-down-dilly has come up to town,
In a yellow petticoat and a green gown.

LITTLE Tommy Tittlemouse,
Lived in a little house;
He caught fishes
In other men's ditches.

ONE foot up, the other foot down,
That's the way to London-town.

THERE was a little boy and a little girl
Lived in an alley;
Says the little boy to the little girl,
"Shall I, oh! shall I?"
Says the little girl to the little boy,
"What shall we do?"
Says the little boy to the little girl,
"I will kiss you!"

LITTLE Bo-peep has lost her sheep,
And can't tell where to find them;
Leave them alone, and they'll come home,
And bring their tails behind them.

JOHNNY shall have a new bonnet,
And Johnny shall go to the fair;
And Johnny shall have a blue ribbon,
To tie up his bonny brown hair.

K.G

JACK and Jill
Went up the hill,
To fetch a pail of water;
Jack fell down
And broke his crown,
And Jill came tumbling after.

BILLY boy blue, come blow me your horn,
The sheeps' in the meadow, the cows'
in the corn;
Is that the way you mind your sheep,
Under the Haycock fast asleep?

HERE am I, little jumping Joan,
When nobody's with me,
I'm always alone.

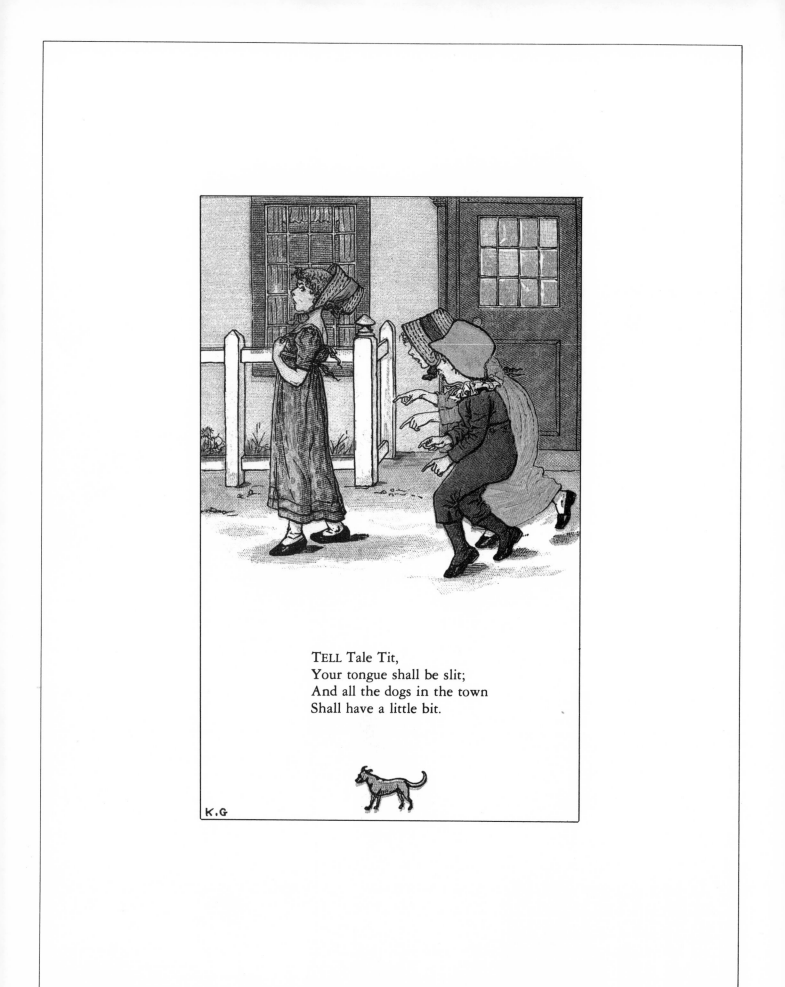

TELL Tale Tit,
Your tongue shall be slit;
And all the dogs in the town
Shall have a little bit.

ROCK-a-bye baby,
Thy cradle is green;
Father's a nobleman,
Mother's a queen.
And Betty's a lady,
And wears a gold ring;
And Johnny's a drummer,
And drums for the king.

LITTLE Tom Tucker,
He sang for his supper.
What did he sing for?
Why, white bread and butter.
How can I cut it without a knife?
How can I marry without a wife?

ELSIE Marley has grown so fine,
She won't get up to serve the swine;
But lies in bed till eight or nine,
And surely she does take her time.

LUCY Locket, lost her pocket,
Kitty Fisher found it;
There was not a penny in it,
But a ribbon round it.

GOOSEY, goosey, gander,
Where shall I wander?
Up stairs, down stairs,
And in my lady's chamber:
There I met an old man,
Would not say his prayrers;
Take him by the left leg,
Throw him down the stairs.

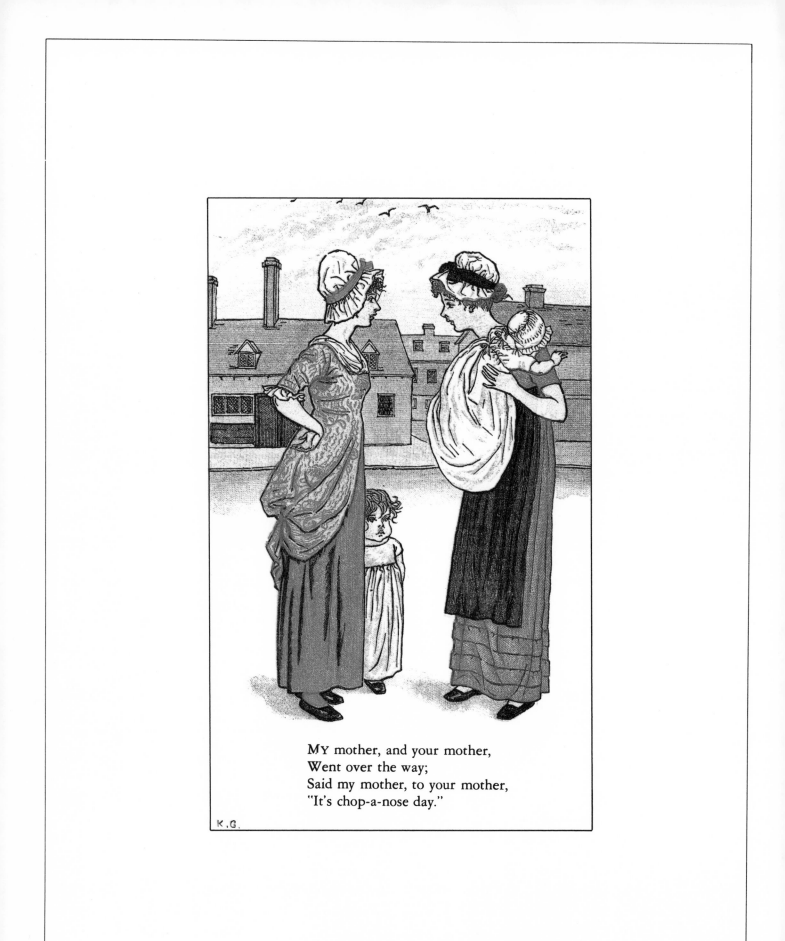

MY mother, and your mother,
Went over the way;
Said my mother, to your mother,
"It's chop-a-nose day."

K.G.

LITTLE Betty Blue,
Lost her holiday shoe.
What will poor Betty do?
Why, give her another,
To match the other,
And then she will walk in two.

A DILLER, a dollar,
A ten o'clock scholar;
What makes you come so soon?
You used to come at ten o'clock,
But now you come at noon!

MARY, Mary, quite contrary,
How does your garden grow?
With silver bells, and cockle shells,
And cowslips all of a row.

LITTLE Miss Muffet,
Sat on a tuffet,
Eating some curds and whey,
There came a great spider,
And sat down beside her,
And frightened Miss Muffet away.

SEE-Saw-Jack in the hedge,
Which is the way to London-bridge?

LITTLE lad, little lad,
Where wast thou born?
Far off in Lancashire,
Under a thorn;
Where they sup sour milk
From a ram's horn.

As Tommy Snooks, and Bessie Brooks
Were walking out one Sunday;
Says Tommy Snooks to Bessie Brooks,
"To-morrow—will be Monday."

GIRLS and boys come out to play,
The moon it shines, as bright as day;
Leave your supper, and leave your sleep,
And come to your playmates in the street;
Come with a whoop, come with a call,
Come with a good will, or come not at all;
Up the ladder and down the wall,
A halfpenny loaf will serve us all.

RING-a-ring-a-roses,
A pocketfull of posies;
Hush! hush! hush! hush!
We're all tumbled down.

KATE GREENAWAY'S
BOOK OF
GAMES

BATTLEDORE & SHUTTLECOCK.

THIS is a most convenient game, because
one solitary individual can find amusement
as well as any number, provided there is a
bat for each player. The object of the game
is to keep the shuttlecock going
as long as possible.

FOLLOW-MY-LEADER.

AN active and daring boy should be chosen as leader, the others follow him one behind the other, as closely as they can, doing as he does, and going where he goes, over gates, stiles, and obstacles of all kinds. If anyone fails in accomplishing any one feat, he takes his place behind the rest. The next one who fails goes behind him, and so the game continues until the leader chooses to stop.

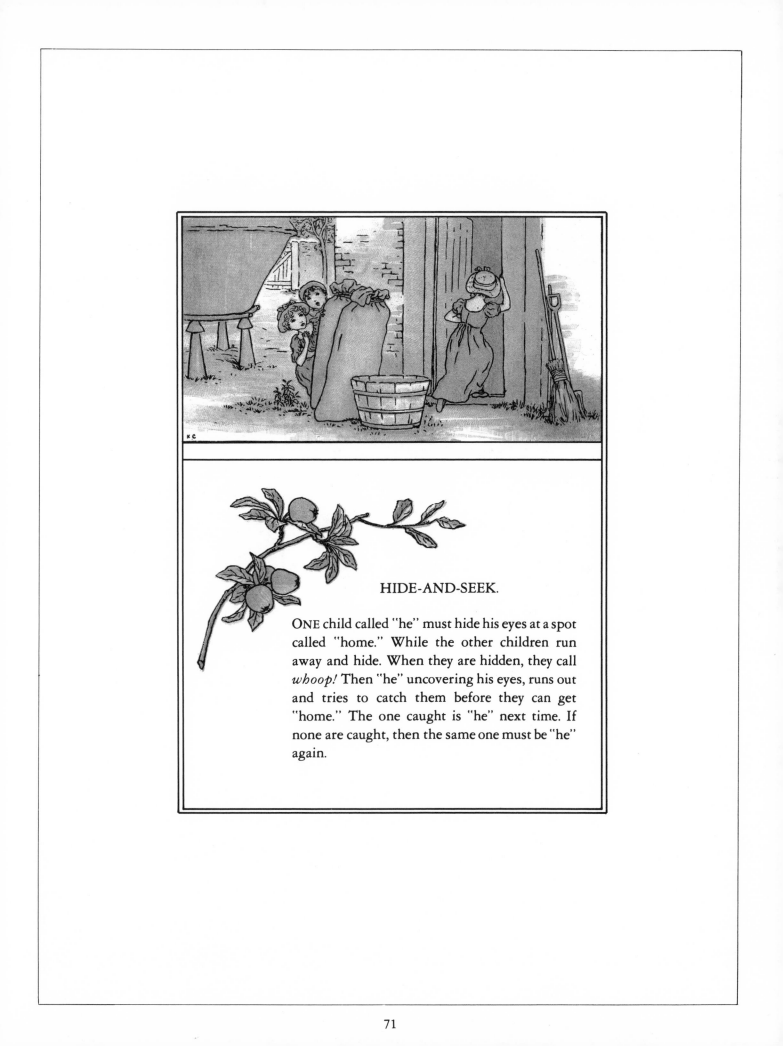

HIDE-AND-SEEK.

ONE child called "he" must hide his eyes at a spot called "home." While the other children run away and hide. When they are hidden, they call *whoop!* Then "he" uncovering his eyes, runs out and tries to catch them before they can get "home." The one caught is "he" next time. If none are caught, then the same one must be "he" again.

MULBERRY BUSH.

THE children form into a ring, and holding hands run round and sing:—

"HERE we go round the mulberry bush,
The mulberry bush, the mulberry bush;
Here we go round the mulberry bush
On a cold and frosty morning."

PUSS IN THE CORNER.

THE child who represents puss stands in the middle, while the others stand at fixed stations round her. One then beckons to another saying: "Puss, puss, give me a drop of water!" when each runs and change places. Puss then runs and tries to get into one of the places, if she succeeds, the one left out is puss.

SEE-SAW.

A GREAT deal of amusement may be derived from having a see-saw. It should be made of a thick plank of wood balanced over a fallen tree-trunk or other suitable erection. The players sit on the ends, balancing themselves as equally as possible, and go up and down. If one player will stand in the middle to work it, he can help to balance it and prevent a sudden jerk should anyone fall or get off without warning.

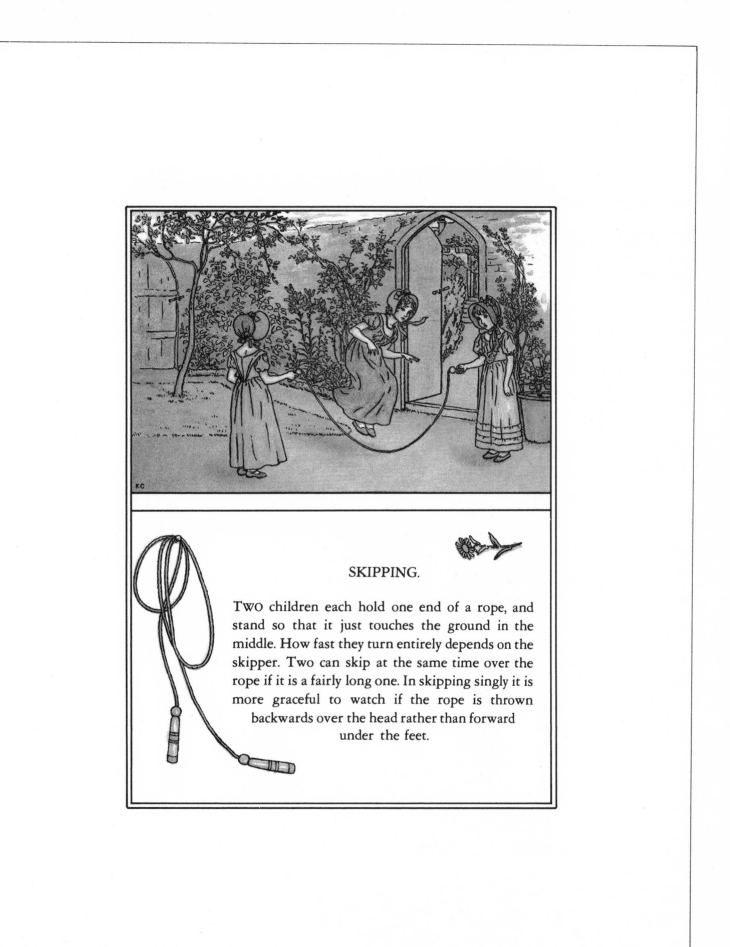

SKIPPING.

TWO children each hold one end of a rope, and
stand so that it just touches the ground in the
middle. How fast they turn entirely depends on the
skipper. Two can skip at the same time over the
rope if it is a fairly long one. In skipping singly it is
more graceful to watch if the rope is thrown
backwards over the head rather than forward
under the feet.

SOAP BUBBLES.

MAKE a lather of soap and warm water, into which dip a clay pipe; blow through it, a bubble then issues from out the bowl—a wonderful transparent globe, glorious with iridescent colors.

SWINGS.

A SWING is a source of much innocent enjoyment which most children can have for a very small outlay. It consists of two upright posts, with a bar securely fastened horizontally; to this two ropes are tied to which a seat is attached. A bough of a tree is a more picturesque place for a swing, but trees are not always to be had for the wishing. Boat swings at fairs are irrestible attractions to most boys.

TOUCH WOOD.

ALL the children but one place themselves in various positions, each touching something that is wood. They keep constantly running from one wooden thing to another. The one left out runs after them, and the first she catches not touching wood takes her place.

MARIGOLD GARDEN

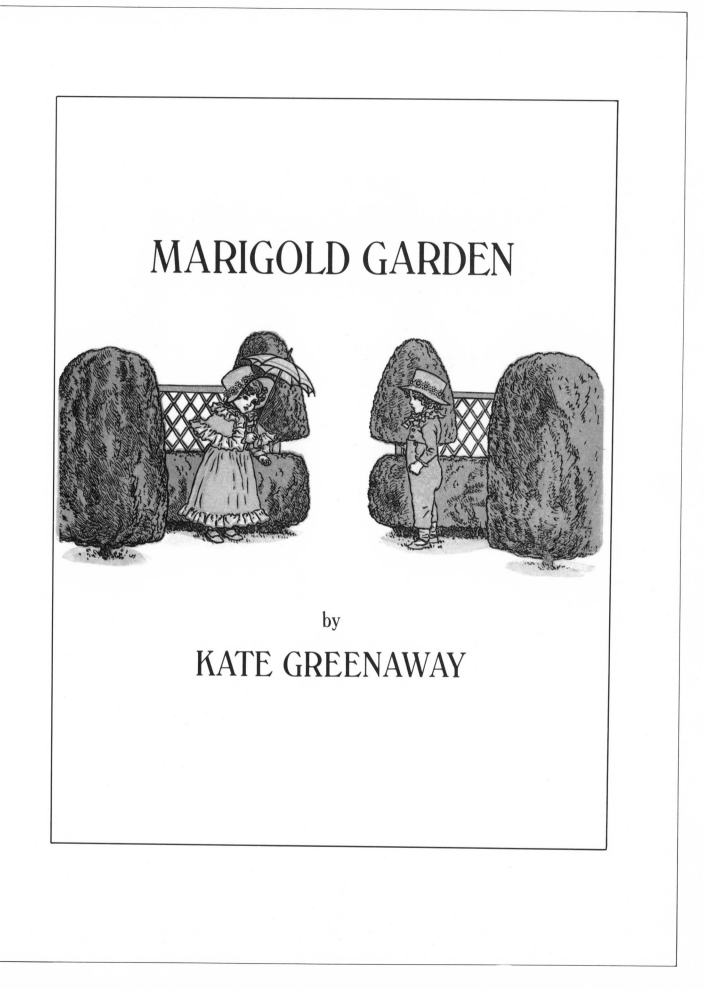

by

KATE GREENAWAY

SUSAN BLUE.

OH, Susan Blue,
How do you do?
Please may I go for a walk with you?
Where shall we go?
Oh, I know—
Down in the meadow where the cowslips grow!

FROM WONDER WORLD.

OUT of Wonder World I think you
    come;
For in your eyes the wonder comes
    with you.
The stars are the windows of Heaven,
And sometimes I think you peep
    through.
Oh, little girl, tell us do the Flowers
Tell you secrets when they find you
    all alone?
Or the Birds and Butterflies whisper
Of things to us unknown?

Or do angel voices speak to you so softly.
When *we* only hear a little wind sigh;
And the peaceful dew of Heaven fall upon you
When *we* only see a white cloud passing by?

TO BABY.

OH, what shall my blue eyes go see?
　　Shall it be pretty Quack-Quack to-day?
Or the Peacock upon the Yew Tree?
　　Or the dear little white Lambs at play?
　　　　Say Baby.
For Baby is such a young Petsy,
　　And Baby is such a sweet Dear.
And Baby is growing quite old now—
　　She's just getting on for a year.

CHILD'S SONG.

THE King and Queen where riding
　　Upon a Summer's day,
And a Blackbird flew above them,
　　To hear what they did say.

The King said he liked apples,
　　The Queen said she liked pears.
And what shall we do to the Blackbird
　　Who listens unawares.

WHEN YOU AND I GROW UP.

WHEN you and I
Grow up—Polly—
  I mean that you and me,
Shall go sailing in a big ship
  Right over all the sea.
We'll wait till we are older,
  For if we went to day,
You know that we might lose ourselves,
  And never find the way.

FIRST ARRIVALS.

IT is a Party, do you know,
And there they sit, all in a row,
Waiting till the others come,
To begin to have some fun.

Hark! the bell rings sharp and clear,
Other little friends appear;
And no longer all alone
They begin to feel at home.

To them a little hard is Fate,
Yet better early than too late;
Fancy getting there forlorn,
With the tea and cake all gone.

Wonder what they'll have for tea;
Hope the jam is strawberry.
Wonder what the dance and game;
Feel so very glad they came.

Very Happy may you be,
May you much enjoy your tea.

ON THE WALL TOP.

DANCING and prancing to town we go,
On the top of the wall of the town we go.
Shall we talk to the stars, or talk to the moon,
Or run along home to our dinner so soon?

ON THE WALL TOP.

SO high—so high on the wall we run,
The nearest the sky—why, the nearer the sun.
If you give me one penny, I'll give you two,
For that's the way good neighbours do.

THE TEA PARTY.

IN the pleasant green Garden
    We sat down to tea;
"Do you take sugar?" and
    "Do you take milk?"
She'd got a new gown on—
    A smart one of silk.
We all were as happy
    As happy could be,
On that bright Summer's day
    When she asked us to tea.

STREET SHOW.

PUFF, puff, puff. How the trumpets blow.
All you little boys and girls come and see
    the show.
One—two—three, the Cat runs up the
    tree;
But the little Bird he flies away—
"She hasn't got me!"

WISHES.

OH, if you were a little boy,
  And I was a little girl—
Why you would have some whiskers grow
  And then my hair would curl.

Ah! if I could have whiskers grow,
  I'd let you have my curls;
But what's the use of wishing it—
  Boys never can be girls.

THE CATS HAVE COME TO TEA.

WHAT did she see—oh, what did she see,
As she stood leaning against the tree?
Why all the Cats had come to tea.

What a fine turn out—from round about,
All the houses had let them out,
And here they were with scamper and shout.

"Mew—mew—mew!" was all the could say,
 And, "We hope we find you well to-day."

Oh, what should she do—oh, what should she do?
What a lot of milk they would get through;
For here they were with "Mew—mew—mew!"

She didn't know—oh, she didn't know,
If bread and butter they'd like or no;
They might want little mice, oh! oh! oh!

Dear me—oh, dear me,
All the cats had come to tea.

TIP-A-TOE.

TIP-A-TOE,
See them go;
One, two, three—
Chloe, Prue, and me;
Up and down,
To the town.
A Lord was there,
And the Lady fair.
And what did they sing?
Oh, "Ring-a-ding-ding;"
And the Black Crow flew off
With the Lady's Ring.

ON THE BRIDGE.

IF I could see a little fish—
That is what I just now wish!
I want to see his great round eyes
Always open in surprise.

I wish a water-rat would glide
Slowly to the other side;
Or a dancing spider sit
On the yellow flags a bit.

I think I'll get some stones to throw
And watch the pretty circles show.
Or shall we sail a flower-boat,
And watch it slowly—slowly float?

That's nice—because you never know
How far away it means to go;
And when to-morrow comes, you see,
It may be in the great wide sea.

BALL.

ONE—two, is one to you;
One—two—three, is one to me.
Throw it fast or not at all,
And mind you do not let it fall.

FAIRY Blue Eyes,
    And Fairy Brown.
And dear little Golden Curls,
    Look down.
I say "Good-bye"—
    "Good-bye" with no pain—
Till some happy day
    We meet again!